IN THE
LAND OF WORDS

NEW AND SELECTED POEMS

BY ELOISE GREENFIELD

ILLUSTRATED BY JAN SPIVEY GILCHRIST

Amistad

ACKNOWLEDGMENTS

Thanks to Antoinette Fogg
Special thanks to my cousin,
Jerlean McAlister, for that
extra hand when I needed it.
Love you
—J.S.G.

Amistad is an imprint of HarperCollins Publishers.

In the Land of Words: New and Selected Poems
Compilation copyright © 2004 by Eloise Greenfield
Illustrations copyright © 2004 by Jan Spivey Gilchrist
Manufactured in China. All rights reserved.
For information address HarperCollins Children's Books,
a division of HarperCollins Publishers, 195 Broadway, New York, NY 10007.
www.harpercollinschildrens.com

Library of Congress Cataloging-in-Publication Data
Greenfield, Eloise.
In the land of words : new and selected poems / by Eloise Greenfield ; illustrated by Jan Spivey Gilchrist.
p.   cm.
Includes index.
ISBN 978-0-06-028993-5 (trade bdg.) — ISBN 978-0-06-028994-2 (lib. bdg.) — ISBN 978-0-06-443692-2 (pbk.)
1. Children's poetry, American.   [1. American poetry.]   I. Gilchrist, Jan Spivey, ill.   II. Title.
PS3557.R39416 I5   2004
811'.54—dc21   2001024599
Typography by Stephanie Bart-Horvath
17 18 19   SCP   20 19 18 17 16 15
❖
First Edition

To Judy Richardson
for the skill and integrity she brings
to her work as a documentarian
and for her friendship
—E.G.

For my sisters, Sular, Mary, Gail, Mable, and Ina,
and in loving memory of Vicki and Melba
—J.S.G.

ALSO BY ELOISE GREENFIELD

Africa Dream, illustrated by Carole Byard

Childtimes: A Three-Generation Memoir,
with Lessie Jones Little and illustrated by Jerry Pinkney

For the Love of the Game: Michael Jordan and Me,
illustrated by Jan Spivey Gilchrist

Honey, I Love and Other Love Poems,
illustrated by Diane and Leo Dillon

Honey, I Love, illustrated by Jan Spivey Gilchrist

How They Got Over: African Americans and the Call of the Sea,
illustrated by Jan Spivey Gilchrist

I Can Draw a Weeposaur and Other Dinosaurs,
illustrated by Jan Spivey Gilchrist

Mary McLeod Bethune, illustrated by Jerry Pinkney

Me & Neesie, illustrated by Jan Spivey Gilchrist

Rosa Parks, illustrated by Gil Ashby

She Come Bringing Me That Little Baby Girl,
illustrated by John Steptoe

Sister, illustrated by Moneta Barnett

Talk About a Family, illustrated by James Calvin

Under the Sunday Tree, illustrated by Amos Ferguson

Water, Water, illustrated by Jan Spivey Gilchrist

William and the Good Old Days,
illustrated by Jan Spivey Gilchrist

AUTHOR'S NOTE

I am often asked by children where my words—the words that I shape into stories and poems—come from. I don't always know the answer.

The words can come from a memory, or a dream, or something I see or hear or wonder about or imagine. But sometimes they just flow into my head and surprise me, and I have no idea how they got there.

Maybe there's a place where words live, where our minds and hearts can go and find them when we want to write—or read.

I like to imagine that there *is* such a place. I call it "The Land of Words."

Won't you come with me now for a visit to this land?

Eloise Greenfield

CONTENTS

In the Land of Words

In the land
of words,
I stand as still
as a tree,
and let the words
rain down on me.
Come, rain, bring
your knowledge and your
music.   Sing
while I grow green
and full.
I'll stand as still
as a tree,
and let your blessings
fall on me.

Part I

The Poet /
The Poem

Nathaniel's Rap

Many children believe that my Nathaniel is real, and he is real—but only in the world of my imagination. I don't know how or why he came to me, but I kept going into that world to see him. I watched him live, I heard him speak. I know him well. I love him.

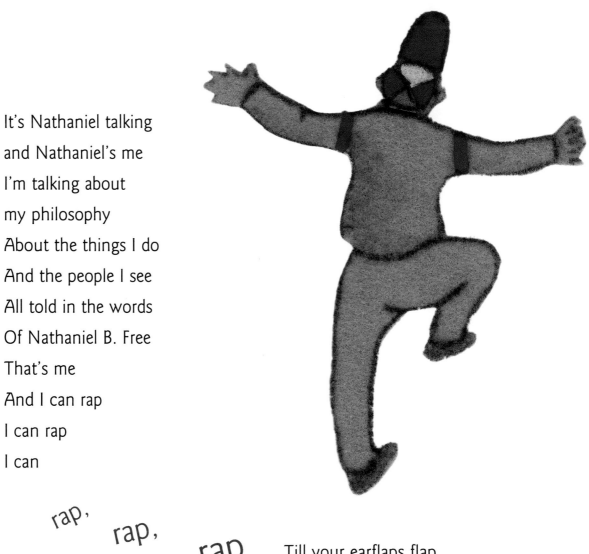

It's Nathaniel talking
and Nathaniel's me
I'm talking about
my philosophy
About the things I do
And the people I see
All told in the words
Of Nathaniel B. Free
That's me
And I can rap
I can rap
I can

rap,   rap,   rap   Till your earflaps flap

I can talk that talk
Till you go for a walk
I can run it on down
Till you get out of town

I can rap

I can rap

Rested, dressed and feeling fine
I've got something on my mind
Friends and kin and neighborhood
Listen now and listen good
Nathaniel's talking
Nathaniel B. Free
Talking about
My philosophy

Been thinking all day
I got a lot to say
Gotta run it on down
Nathaniel's way
Okay!
I gotta rap
Gotta rap
Gotta rap, rap, rap
Till your earflaps flap
Gotta talk that talk
Till you go for a walk
Gotta run it on down
Till you get out of town

Gotta rap
Gotta rap

Rested, dressed and feeling fine
I've got something on my mind
Friends and kin and neighborhood
Listen now and listen good

I'm gonna rap, hey!
Gonna rap, hey!
Gonna rap, hey!
I'm gonna rap!

To Catch a Fish

This poem was inspired by a painting by Amos Ferguson.
I thought of the patience it takes to go fishing.

It takes more than a wish
to catch a fish
you take the hook
you add the bait
you concentrate
and then you wait
you wait   you wait
but not a bite
the fish don't have
an appetite
so tell them what
good bait you've got
and how your bait
can hit the spot
this works a whole
lot better than
a wish
if you really
want to catch
a fish

Keepsake

When I was a small child, one of my neighbors, a very kind man, died. His wife gave me a penny when she saw how sad I was. She said it was a gift from him, but I think now that it may have been a gift from her, that she put her own sadness aside for a moment to try to comfort a child. In writing the poem, I changed the details but tried to capture the feeling.

Before Mrs. Williams died
She told Mr. Williams
When he gets home
To get a nickel out of her
Navy blue pocketbook
And give it to her
Sweet little gingerbread girl
That's me

I ain't never going to spend it

New Baby Poem (I)

I was thinking about how a new little baby
might feel in a big crib, a big room, a big world.

all day she has slept
now is her time
to cry
"Where am I?
I'm too tiny a girl
for this big new world."

New Baby Poem (II)

What do babies dream about?
They can't tell us. I tried to guess.

sleep coming down
bringing dreams that
swish
like the sound of
warm water
rocking the baby
rocking the baby
Swish, swish,
swish.

Way Down in the Music

I love music. There are times when I feel as if I'm down inside the music, it's swirling over my head and all around me, and nothing exists in the whole world, except the music and me.

I get way down in the music
Down inside the music
I let it wake me
            take me
Spin me around and make me
Uh-get down

Inside the sound of the Jackson Five
Into the tune of Earth, Wind and Fire
Down in the bass where the beat comes from
Down in the horn and down in the drum
I get down
I get down

I get way down in the music
Down inside the music
I let it wake me
                take me
Spin me around and shake me
I get down, down
I get down

Making Friends

When my son was in kindergarten, he was fascinated that one of his class-mates could imitate a rabbit. She'd make long ears by sticking her fingers up on her head, she'd shape her mouth like a rabbit's, and top it all off by wiggling her nose.

when I was in kindergarten

    this new girl came in our class one day

        and the teacher told her to sit beside me

        and I didn't know what to say

            so I wiggled my nose and made my bunny face

          and she laughed

              then she puffed out her cheeks

              and she made a funny face

              and I laughed

              so then

                  we were friends

Flowers

Jan Spivey Gilchrist sent me a drawing she had done of her husband and her daughter. She asked if I would write a poem about stepfathers. As I looked at the drawing, I could see and feel the love and care of a father, and the words came.

My stepfather brought me flowers today.
For my first solo—my first bouquet,

yellow **and** peach
and purple and red,

"Daughter, you sang like an angel," he said.
My stepfather brought me flowers, and I
pretended there wasn't a tear in his eye,
flowers and happiness tied with a bow,
because I had just sung my first solo.

Excerpt from Family

These are childhood memories. When I began writing them, I used many words and I punctuated them in the usual way. But the memories didn't run one into the other the way memories often do in our thoughts. I kept going back to the page, crossing out words, and more words, and periods and commas, until I found the feeling I wanted.

Saturday Sunday mornings

Daddy making pancakes

big as the plate Daddy

making fat hamburgers

leftover stuffed with rice

green peas enough for

everybody. . . . Lincoln Park

evenings Mama other mothers

bench-talk children playing. . . .

Downtown Wilbur Gerald Eloise

wait in the car have fun get

mad have fun get mad. . . . Vedie

little sister turning somersaults

we laugh. Vera baby sister

sweet baby laughing we laugh. . . .

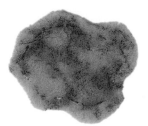

Parade take turns on Daddy's

shoulder watch the floats

watch the firemen march

watch the horns watch

the sound of the bass

drum. . . . Easter Monday picnic

zoo dyed eggs lionhouse

popcorn polar bear picnic.

Merry-go-round Mama laughing.

Sparrow's Beach sun

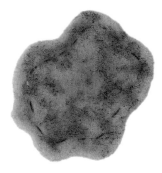

water-splashing sandy legs

Mama laughing.

mama laughing. . . .

Family.

Part II

In the Land

Books

I've got
Books on the bunk bed
Books on the chair
Books on the couch
And every old where

But I want more books
I just can't get enough
I want more books about
All kinds of stuff, like

      Jackie's troubles
      Raymond's joys
      Rabbits, kangaroos
      Girls and boys
      Mountains, valleys
      Winter, spring
      Campfires, vampires
      Every old thing

I want to

Lie down on my bunk bed

Lean back in my chair

Curl up on the couch

And every old where

And
read
more
books!

Story

I step into the story,
I leave my world behind,
I let the walls of story
Be the walls around my mind.

New faces and new voices,
I listen and I see,
and people I have never met
mean everything to me.

I worry when they worry,
I quake when danger's near,
I hold my breath and hope
that all their troubles disappear.

I don't know what will happen,
I never know what I'll find,
when I step into a story
and leave my world behind.

Twister

He can't say it,
she can't say it.
Can I say it?
No.

We have to say it
fast, of course,
no fair to say it slow.
It twists our tongues,
it twists our brains,
our faces start to frown.
But I bet it would be
a bit better, buddies—
if we could slow it down.
Come on, let's slow it
down.

Jokes

Every day we get together
to see who can tell
the funniest joke.
We don't even have to vote.

It's always Crystal
who wins.

The words come flying
out of her mouth,
straight to the center
of our funny bones,
tickling us into
losing the game
and loving it.

Riddles

The ones I like the most
are the ones that make you
think and think,
while everybody waits,
hoping you'll give up.

Give up? Not me.

I'll get it.
You'll see.

Poet/Poem

Poet: Where are you, words,
the ones that will fit
the thoughts I am thinking,
as here I sit?

Poem: Hiding, I'm hiding,
I let you see
only the smallest
part of me.
If you want to see more,
you'll have to go deep
into the forest
where I sleep.

Poet: But suppose I get lost?
Poem: You might.
Poet: I'm afraid.
Poem: All right. Good-bye.
Poet: Wait! Don't go.
I'll try.

Poem

Poem, you caught me
by surprise,
took me inside
stormy skies,
flashing light
and rain and thunder
ripped the cloud
I hovered under,
then the sun
burst out to say,
"Get back, storm,
you're in my way!"
What a brightness,
what a glow,
thank you, Poem,
for such a show,
and when I am
back at home,
I won't forget you,
Poem.

Two Poems

The first one made me
smile a bit,
laugh out loud
at the end of it.

The next one almost
made me cry.
Did the butterfly
have to die?

Two poems entered
magically,
and touched two places
inside of me.

Oh, Words

Oh, I love those wacky words,
those crazy words that crack me up,
like *dibbily-doobily-doo* and such,
they don't mean much,
but oh, I love them so.

Oh, I love those wicked words,
those mean, mean words
from the mouths of sorcerers,
who point and yell
and cast a spell, saying,
"You will sleep for a thousand
 years,
 I will not change,
  so stop your tears. *Sleep!*"
  And the good folks fall
   and then lie still,
   while I hug myself
   to hold the chill
   brought on by those
   wicked words.

Oh, I love those yucky words,
those words that make me
see and smell the goo.
Ooh! It's gross, it's awful
and it's bad!
The yuckiest time I've ever had.

Words, oh, words,
Oh, what a mess,
Wicked, wacky, yucky,
Yes!

I Don't Care

When I go shopping with my big brother,
He tries on one shirt after another,
But I don't ever really care,
As long as I have a book and a chair.

On a family ride that's many miles long,
I don't sing that boredom song,
I never say, "Are we almost there?"
I have my book, and I don't care.

A minute ago, Mama tried to tease,
"John, come look! A dancing cheese!"
I didn't laugh, I didn't look,
My head is buried in my book.

Later, I'll think of a cheese with eyes,
Nose and mouth and legs and thighs,
A cheese that tangos down the stair,
But right now, I just don't care!

I Go to the Land

I go to the land of words,
for I am at home there,
and never leave
for long. My thirst
pushes me through
the open door.
The more I drink
of the falling water,
the more I know.
I drink. I think.
I grow.

SOURCES

"Books" from Children's Book Council bookmark. Copyright © 1979 by Eloise Greenfield.

Excerpt from "Family" from *Childtimes: A Three-Generation Memoir* (HarperCollins [originally T. Y. Crowell]). Copyright © 1979 by Eloise Greenfield and Lessie Jones Little.

"Flowers" from *Angels* (Hyperion Books for Children). Copyright © 1999 by Eloise Greenfield.

"In the Land of Words" from Coretta Scott King Award thirtieth anniversary poster (Hyperion Books for Children). Copyright © 1999 by Eloise Greenfield.

"Keepsake" and "Way Down in the Music" from *Honey, I Love* (HarperCollins [originally T. Y. Crowell]). Copyright © 1978 by Eloise Greenfield.

"Making Friends" and "Nathaniel's Rap" from *Nathaniel Talking* (Black Butterfly Children's Books). Copyright © 1988 by Eloise Greenfield.

"New Baby (I)" and "New Baby (II)" from *Night on Neighborhood Street* (Dial Books for Young Readers). Copyright © 1991 by Eloise Greenfield.

"Poem" from Children's Book Council bookmark. Copyright © 1999 by Eloise Greenfield.

"To Catch a Fish" from *Under the Sunday Tree* (HarperCollins). Copyright © 1988 by Eloise Greenfield.

INDEX

ELOISE GREENFIELD's love of writing shines through brilliantly in each and every one of her books, which include *Honey, I Love and Other Love Poems* and *How They Got Over: African Americans and the Call of the Sea*, both illustrated by Jan Spivey Gilchrist. She is the recipient of the Coretta Scott King Award, the Foundation for Children's Literature Hope S. Dean Award, and the National Council for the Social Studies Carter G. Woodson Book Award. Ms. Greenfield lives in Washington, DC. You can follow her on Twitter @ELGreenfield.

JAN SPIVEY GILCHRIST is the award-winning illustrator-author of seventy-four children's books. Dr. Gilchrist illustrated the highly acclaimed picture book *The Great Migration: Journey to the North*, winner of the Coretta Scott King Honor Award, a Junior Library Guild Best Book, an NAACP Image Award nominee, a CCBC Best Book, and a Georgia State Children's Book Award nominee. She won the Coretta Scott King Award for her illustrations in *Nathaniel Talking* and a Coretta Scott King Honor for her illustrations in *Night on Neighborhood Street*, all written by Eloise Greenfield. She was inducted into the Society of Illustrators in 2001 and into the International Literary Hall of Fame for Writers of African Descent in 1999. She lives near Chicago, Illinois.

The words can come from a memory, or a dream,
or something I see or hear or wonder about or imagine. . . .
Maybe there's a place where words live, where our
minds and hearts can go and find them when we want
to write or read.

I like to imagine that there *is* such a place. I call it
"The Land of Words."

In this collection of twenty-one poems, NCTE Excellence in Poetry for
Children Award winner Eloise Greenfield journeys to a place where words,
creativity, and imagination abound. Featuring the poems "In the Land of
Words," "Books," and "Poem," as well as favorites such as "Nathaniel's
Rap" and "Way Down in the Music," this tribute to the written word
invites readers to look within themselves and discover what inspires them.

Amistad
An Imprint of HarperCollins Publishers
Cover art © 2004 by Jan Spivey Gilchrist
Cover design by Stephanie Bart-Horvath

www.harpercollinschildrens.com
BOOK NEWS, GAMES, CONTESTS, AND MORE

USA **$7.99** / $9.99 CAN
ISBN 978-0-06-443692-2

9 780064 436922
50799

BUZZ ALDRIN

REACHING FOR THE MOON

PAINTINGS BY
WENDELL MINOR